Maya

Her realm: Spring

Her personality: shy and sweet

Her passion: cooking

Her gift: the Power of Heat

Cora

Her realm: Winter

Her personality: proud and sincere

Her passion: ice-skating

Her gift: the Power of Cold

Selena

Her realm: Night

Her personality: deep and sensitive

Her passion: music

Her gift: the Power of Darkness

PAPERCUTZ

Time to Fly

Script by Cortney Powell
Art by Ryan Jampole
MELOWY created by Danielle Star

PAPERCUTZ
New York

MELOWY

MELOWY #3
"Time to Fly"

Cover by RYAN JAMPOLE
Editorial supervision by ALESSANDRA BERELLO and LISA CAPIOTTO (Atlantyca S.p.A.)
Script by CORTNEY POWELL
Art by RYAN JAMPOLE
Color by LAURIE E. SMITH
Lettering by WILSON RAMOS JR.

Production—JAYJAY JACKSON
Managing Editor—JEFF WHITMAN
Editorial Intern—KARR ANTUNES
JIM SALICRUP
Editor-in-Chief

Hardcover ISBN 978-1-5458-0309-7
Paperback ISBN 978-1-5458-0359-2

Printed in India
June 2019

Papercutz books may be purchased for business or promotional use. For information on bulk purchases, please contact Macmillan Corporate and Premium Sales Department at (800) 221-7945 x5442.

Distributed by Macmillan
First Printing

DESTINY, THE CASTLE ABOVE THE CLOUDS, IN A PLACE KNOWN AS AURA...
HERE FLOATS THE SCHOOL FOR MELOWIES, WHERE THE FLYING PEGASUS LEARN ABOUT THEIR HIDDEN POWERS AND DISCOVER THEIR PATHS...
...AND AT DESTINY, ANYTHING IS POSSIBLE....
...THERE IS A TIME FOR EVERYTHING...
...A TIME FOR TESTS...
...A TIME FOR FASHION...

...A TIME TO DANCE...
...AND WE MOST CERTAINLY CANNOT FORGET...
A TIME TO FLY!
TWEEEE

IT ALL STARTED DURING OUR TIME TO *EAT,* WHEN *PRINCIPAL GIA* ADDRESSED THE STUDENTS...
I AM PLEASED TO ANNOUNCE THAT THE *AEROBATIC TOURNAMENT* IS ALMOST UPON US. THE COMPETITION IS GOING TO BE AN EXCITING AND CHALLENGING *THREE DAYS* THAT NONE OF YOU WILL EVER FORGET!
THE TRYOUTS, TO QUALIFY TO BE ON THE TEAM OF SIX, WILL TAKE PLACE WITH *MS. MERCURY*...AND THEY WILL BE BASED ON *SPEED, GRACE,* AND *CREATIVITY!*
GASP! I HAVE ALWAYS *DREAMED* OF BEING IN THE AEROBATIC TOURNAMENT!
WE ARE NOT JUST GOING TO BE IN IT, *CLEO!* WE ARE GOING TO WIN IT!
OF COURSE, I WANT YOU *ALL* TO HAVE FUN, BUT DO NOT FORGET THIS IS A *SERIOUS SPORT....*
YOU THINK YOU CAN HANDLE THAT, *ELECTRA?!*
HA! I CAN BE *SERIOUS, CORA!*

CLEO, ELECTRA, AND CORA ARE PRACTICALLY ALREADY ON THE TEAM!
ARE YOU GOING TO TRYOUT, SELENA?
AND HAVE OUR WHOLE SCHOOL WATCHING ME FLY AROUND? NO THANKS!
I'D RATHER BE BAKING IN A KITCHEN WITH YOU, MAYA!
THAT CAN BE ARRANGED!
THE COMPETITION WILL BE MORE CHALLENGING THAN YOU CAN IMAGINE!
IT'LL BE A PIECE OF CAKE FOR ME!
WE ARE BY FAR THE BEST AT FLYING, KATE!
I MUST MODESTLY AGREE, ERIS.
MS. MERCURY, YOU CAN TAKE IT FROM HERE...
MELOWIES, IF YOU WANT TO TRYOUT...

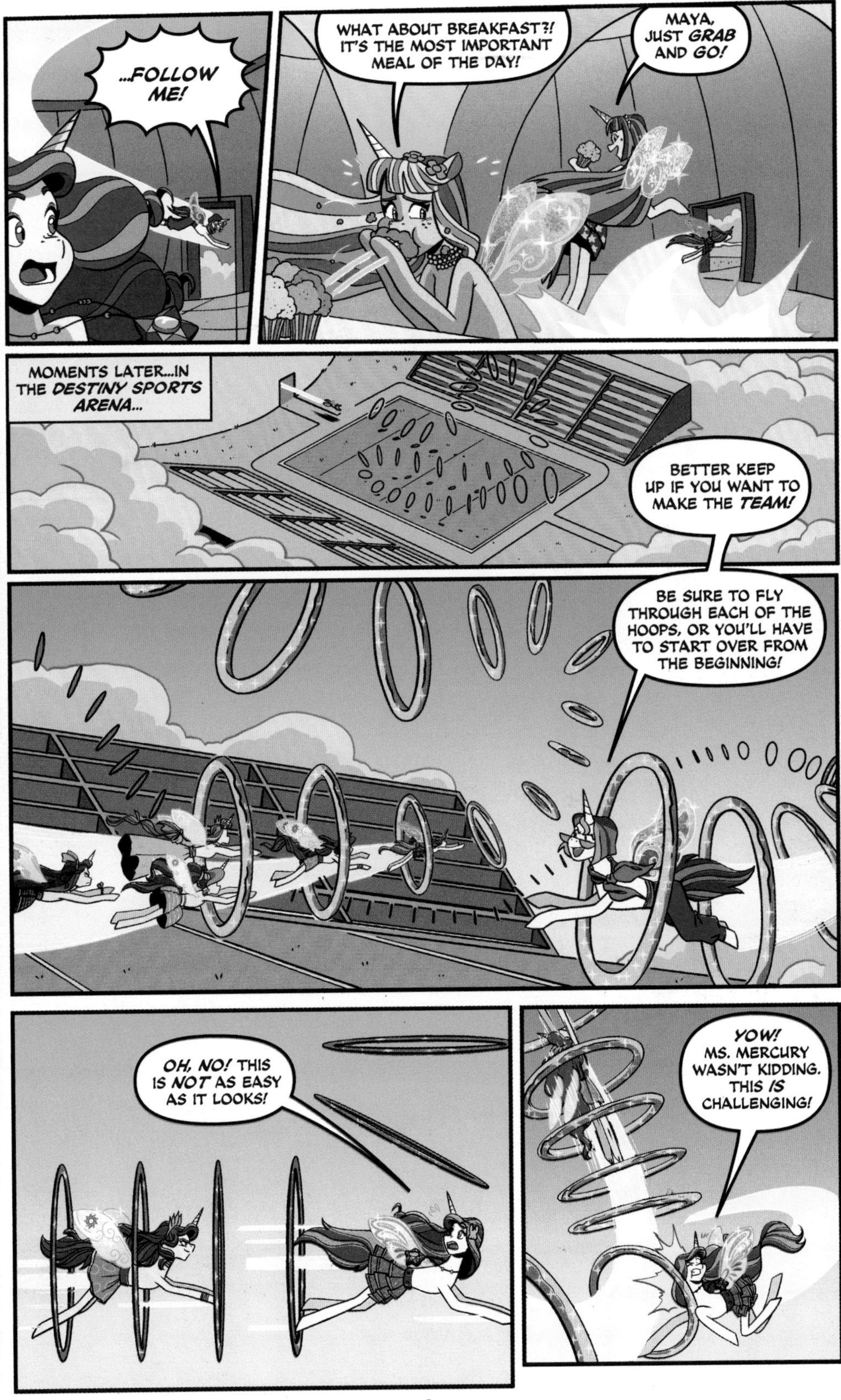
...FOLLOW ME!
WHAT ABOUT BREAKFAST?! IT'S THE MOST IMPORTANT MEAL OF THE DAY!
MAYA, JUST GRAB AND GO!
MOMENTS LATER...IN THE DESTINY SPORTS ARENA...
BETTER KEEP UP IF YOU WANT TO MAKE THE TEAM!
BE SURE TO FLY THROUGH EACH OF THE HOOPS, OR YOU'LL HAVE TO START OVER FROM THE BEGINNING!
OH, NO! THIS IS NOT AS EASY AS IT LOOKS!
YOW! MS. MERCURY WASN'T KIDDING. THIS IS CHALLENGING!

I'M STARTING OVER...
LAST PLACE IS BETTER THAN NO PLACE. SO, HERE I GO AGAIN!
⩲MUNCH!⩱ YOU CAN DO IT, CLEO!
⩲GULP!⩱ WE BELIEVE IN YOU, CLEO!
ONE LAST HOOP TO GO...
...THE HOOP OF FIRE!...
...WHO IS BRAVE ENOUGH?
YOU WANT US TO GO THROUGH THAT?!
ISN'T THAT DANGEROUS?
I'LL DO IT!

CLEO! YOU MADE IT!
AND NOW I'M READY FOR THE HOOP OF FIRE!
I DIDN'T SAY I WASN'T GOING TO DO IT...BUT I HARDLY THINK IT WOULD BE SAFE FOR A MELOWY WHO CAN'T EVEN STAY INSIDE THE HOOPS!
YOU'RE RIGHT, ERIS. THAT WOULD NOT BE SAFE FOR ANY OF YOU, BUT THAT WASN'T THE REAL TEST...
IT IS ONE THING TO STAY IN THE CIRCLE AND GO THROUGH THE HOOPS, IT IS QUITE ANOTHER TO PICK YOURSELF UP AFTER FALLING OUT!
THAT TAKES DETERMINATION. CLEO PASSED THE FIRST TEST! WELCOME TO THE DESTINY AEROBATIC TEAM, CLEO!
GASP! I-I'M ON THE TEAM?!
FOR THE REST OF YOU, HAVE NO FEAR, AFTER I AM DONE WITH YOU, IT'LL BE A PIECE OF CAKE. RIGHT, KATE?
UM... RIGHT...
SECOND DAY OF TRYOUTS BEGIN TOMORROW!

THE NEXT DAY, THE TRYOUTS CONTINUE...WITH ALL DIFFERENT TYPES OF HOOPS TO FLY THROUGH...
HOOPS OF MAGICAL WATER, THAT STOP MELOWIES FROM FLYING...
OH, NO! LOOK OUT BELOW!
...HOOPS THAT CHANGE SIZES...
BOP
OW!
... HOOPS THAT CHANGE COURSE...
HEY! NOT FAIR!
...RINGS THAT DISAPPEAR...
MS. MERCURY HAS US LITERALLY JUMPING THROUGH HOOPS TO GET ON THE TEAM!
THIS IS TOO EASY!
...AND REAPPEAR SOMEWHERE ELSE....
HEY, THAT'S MY HOOP! THIS IS RIDICULOUS!
HEE HEE.
THE LAST CHALLENGE WAS MAINLY TO TEST YOUR SKILLS FOR HANDLING STRESS...
...ANGER WILL ALWAYS GET IN THE WAY OF FOCUS, WHICH IS KEY IN AEROBATICS!
WHAT'S THE POINT, IF YOU CAN'T WIN?

THE POINT ISN'T IN WINNING, MY DEAR ERIS...
MS. MERCURY'S HEARING IS SURPRISINGLY GOOD!
THE POINT IS IN PLAYING THE GAME... WINNING MEANS, THE GAME IS OVER.
GASP!
OOOOO!
...WHICH BRINGS US TO OUR NEXT CHALLENGE...
...LIGHTNING DODGE BALL!
HEY! MAYBE A LITTLE WARNING NEXT TIME?
WHOA!
ELECTRA, THINK FAST!

THE TRYOUTS FLY BY AND THE DAY FINALLY ARRIVES FOR MS. MERCURY TO PICK THE REST OF DESTINY'S AEROBATIC TEAM...
ALL OF YOU WERE EXCEPTIONAL, BUT UNFORTUNATELY ONLY SIX MEMBERS ARE ALLOWED ON EACH TEAM...
THE NEW TEAM MEMBERS ARE...
ELECTRA...
CORA...
CLEO...
KATE...
XENI...
...AND LEDA!
GASP!
...FOR THE REST OF YOU, JUST BECAUSE YOU CAN'T FLY IN THE COMPETITION, DOES NOT MEAN YOU ARE NOT A PART OF THIS TOURNAMENT...EVERYONE AT DESTINY IS A PART OF THIS EXPERIENCE, WHERE MELOWY STRENGTH, COURAGE, ENDURANCE, AND LOVE FOR FLYING IS EXPRESSED TO THE FULLEST!
ERIS DOES NOT HANDLE REJECTION WELL...

SNIFF! IT ISN'T FAIR, IT ISN'T FAIR!
SNIFF! THOSE FILLIES GET EVERYTHING AND I GET NOTHING!
CIRCE, I NEED YOUR HELP!
ERIS, ARE YOU OKAY?
I NEVER SAID I WOULDN'T JUMP THROUGH THAT HOOP OF FIRE, SOB! BUT MS. MERCURY CHOSE CLEO INSTEAD OF ME! I TRY TO BE GOOD AND POSITIVE, BUT SOB! THOSE FILLIES ALWAYS GET IN MY WAY!
CLEO SEEMS TO BE THE MAIN CAUSE OF YOUR PROBLEM...BUT I HAVE JUST THE THING!

I'M TRYING TO STAY AWAY FROM CHEATING OR ANY SPELLS BECAUSE OF WHAT HAPPENED LAST TIME...*
I GUESS I JUST WANTED SOMEONE TO TALK TO...
I HATE TO SEE SOMEONE SO TALENTED AND SMART BE TREATED SO POORLY...
EXACTLY!
SNIFF! THANK YOU, CIRCE, YOU ALWAYS MAKE ME FEEL BETTER...
SOMETIMES THERE IS NOTHING WRONG WITH USING AN INNOCENT SPELL TO HELP YOUR TALENT SHINE...AND POSSIBLY HELP THAT FILLY, CLEO, BE MORE HUMBLE!
UM... I DON'T KNOW...

*ERIS IS REFERRING TO THE TIME SHE NEARLY DESTROYED THE NEON FOREST WITH A MAGICAL PAINTBRUSH, DURING THE FASHION CLUB TRYOUTS. SEE *MELOWY #2.*

MEANWHILE AT THE DESTINY DORM...
CONGRATULATIONS!
CONGRATULATIONS!
GASP!
♫ GET READY ♫ FOR CLEO... ELECTRA... AND CORAAAAA!
♫ THEY ARE GOING TO FLY SO HIIIIIIGH! ♫
♫ THE MEGASES FROM CHANCE... DON'T STAND ♫ A CHANCE! ♫
YOU SING IT, SELENA!
HAHAHAHAHA!
REMEMBER IT'S NOT ABOUT WINNING... JUST KIDDING!
HA! TELL THAT TO THE MEGAS!
THE MELOWIES WILL GET THEIR CHANCE TO DO THAT, WHEN DAYS LATER THE TEAM OF CHANCE ARRIVES...
MEGAS, PREPARE FOR OUR DATE WITH DESTINY! ARE YOU READY, TEAM?
YOU KNOW IT, COACH!
READY, GIRLS?
TIME FOR A MEET AND GREET...

SELENA ISN'T THAT YOUR BEST MEGAS FRIEND, TOBY?!
YES, IT IS!
DID YOU KNOW HE WAS COMING?
HAHAHA! I MIGHT HAVE...
AND, BOY IS HE GOING TO BE GLAD TO SEE YOU!
ALL AT ONCE, MEMORIES OF HER VISIT TO THE NIGHT REALM, WHICH IS WHERE SELENA IS FROM, FLASH THROUGH CLEO'S MIND...
AN EXPERIENCE SHE WILL NEVER FORGET...
SHE GOT TO MEET SELENA'S MOTHER, QUEEN NEMESIS...
SHE GOT TO ATTEND HER FIRST BALL...

BUT THE MOST MEMORABLE PART WAS MEETING *TOBY*...
...THEIR FRIENDSHIP GREW FAST...
...INTO SOMETHING MORE *MAGICAL* THAN ALL THE FANCY JEWELS AT THE PALACE.
CLEO ISN'T THE ONLY MELOWY, HOWEVER, WHO CAN'T TAKE HER EYES OFF TOBY...
SNICKER! ERIS, YOU LOOK *LOVE-STRUCK!*
I HAVE A NEW *CALLING!*
BIT LATER, AS LEDA, ATE, AND ERIS HEAD ARDS THE CAFETERIA R THE *WELCOMING FEAST*...
THAT DARK HAIRED *MEGAS* IS *DREAMY*...
I THINK ERIS WOULD DISAGREE...HAHA! I SAW WHO *YOU* WERE STARING AT!
YOU FILLIES MAY THINK YOU CAN FLY BETTER THAN ME, BUT I KNOW THAT I CAN *FLIRT* BETTER THAN ANY MELOWY!

YOU HAVE AN AWESOME SCHOOL!
THE STAFF TRANSFORMED THE CAFETERIA INTO A MYSTICAL CANDLELIT DINING HALL! AFTER DINNER WE HAVE TO TAKE YOU ON A GRAND TOUR OF DESTINY...
BUT FIRST WE MUST PLAY A GAME OF FLY AND SEEK!
OW!
SORRY, THERE WAS A WEED FROM WHEN YOU RAN INTO THAT TREE AT PRACTICE...
HEY, I'M ERIS...YOU SHOULD SIT WITH ME AND I CAN TELL YOU ALL ABOUT HOW CLEO TRICKED MS. MERCURY INTO LETTING HER BE ON THE TEAM...
UM, ERIS, THIS IS MY BEST FRIEND TOBY, FROM THE NIGHT REALM!
I'M SURE YOU MEANT TO SAY, YOU WANT TO TELL HOW CLEO, BECAUSE OF HER BRAVERY, WAS CHOSEN FIRST TO BE ON THE TEAM!
IT WAS A PLEASURE MEETING YOU, ERIS, BUT CAN I TAKE A RAIN CHECK, SO I CAN CATCH UP WITH MY FRIENDS?
OKAY, BUT IF YOU GET BORED, COME FIND ME!

TO A MAGNIFICENT BEGINNING OF THE AEROBATIC TOURNAMENT BETWEEN CHANCE AND DESTINY, A GAME THAT I HOPE BRINGS OUT THE BEST IN ALL THE PLAYERS!
MAY THE BEST FLYER WIN!
FINALLY...
MELOWIES AND MEGAS, WELCOME TO THE FIRST DAY OF...
...THE AEROBATIC TOURNAMENT...
EACH OF YOU WILL GO THROUGH A FLYATHLON!
THE WINNER WILL BE BASED ON SPEED AND ACCURACY!

SOME THINGS TO KEEP IN MIND...DON'T GET WET, DON'T TOUCH THE GROUND, DON'T BURN YOURSELF AND...TIMING IS EVERYTHING! SO WITHOUT ANY FURTHER ADO...
LET THE GAMES BEGIN!
I'M SO NERVOUS! I FEEL LIKE I'M COMPETING!
LOOK HOW CLEO AND TOBY LOOK AT EACH OTHER...NEVER THOUGHT I'D BE A MATCHMAKER.
GO, AERIES!
OH, NO!
I DIDN'T EVEN MAKE IT THROUGH THE FIRST RING!
GO, LEDA!
I MADE IT THROUGH THE WATERFALL RING...
...BUT I'M NOT SURE ABOUT THOSE LIMBO VINES UP NEXT!
WHOAAAAA!
SSWWLLIPP

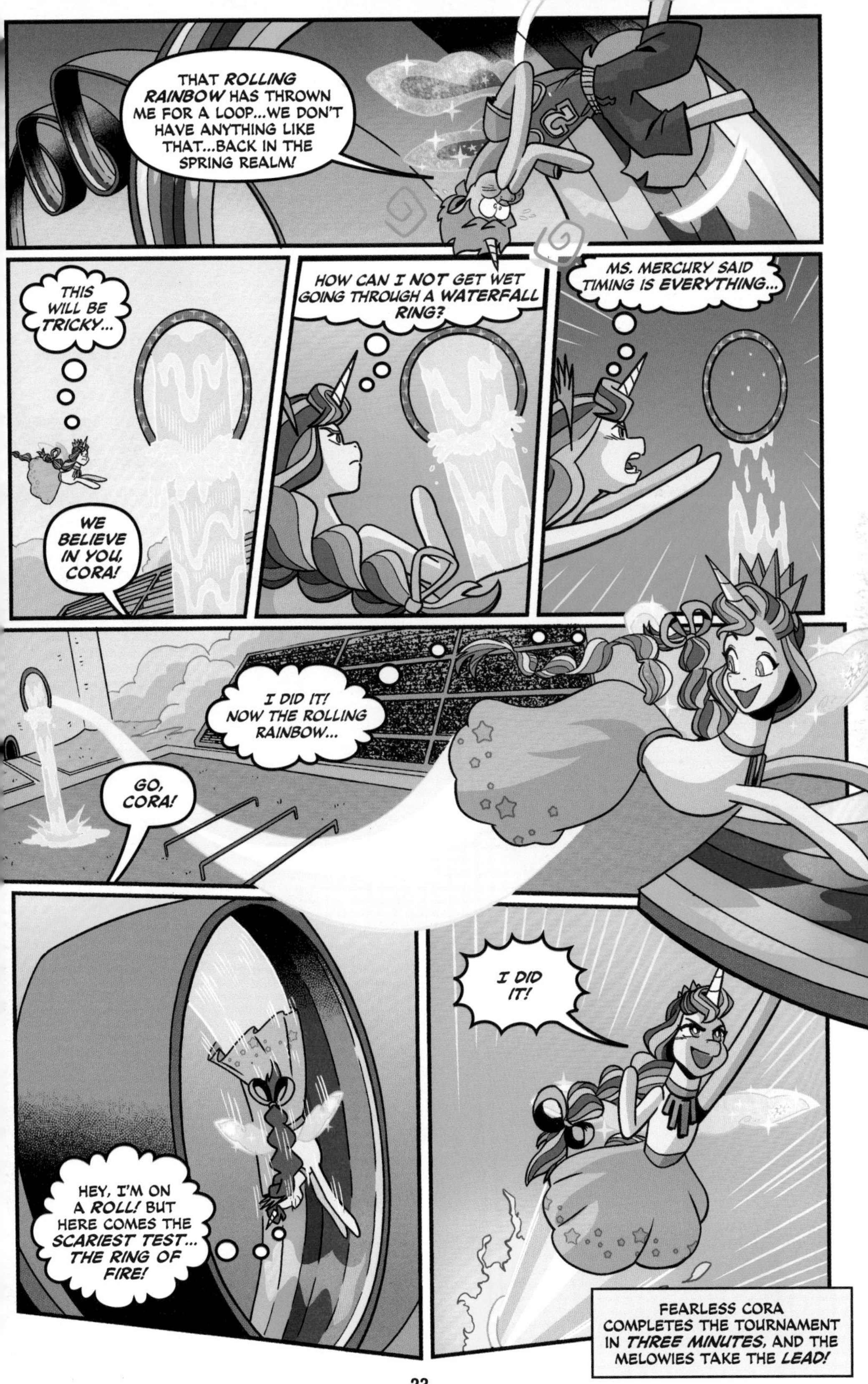
THAT ROLLING RAINBOW HAS THROWN ME FOR A LOOP...WE DON'T HAVE ANYTHING LIKE THAT...BACK IN THE SPRING REALM!
THIS WILL BE TRICKY...
WE BELIEVE IN YOU, CORA!
HOW CAN I NOT GET WET GOING THROUGH A WATERFALL RING?
MS. MERCURY SAID TIMING IS EVERYTHING...
I DID IT! NOW THE ROLLING RAINBOW...
GO, CORA!
HEY, I'M ON A ROLL! BUT HERE COMES THE SCARIEST TEST... THE RING OF FIRE!
I DID IT!
FEARLESS CORA COMPLETES THE TOURNAMENT IN THREE MINUTES, AND THE MELOWIES TAKE THE LEAD!

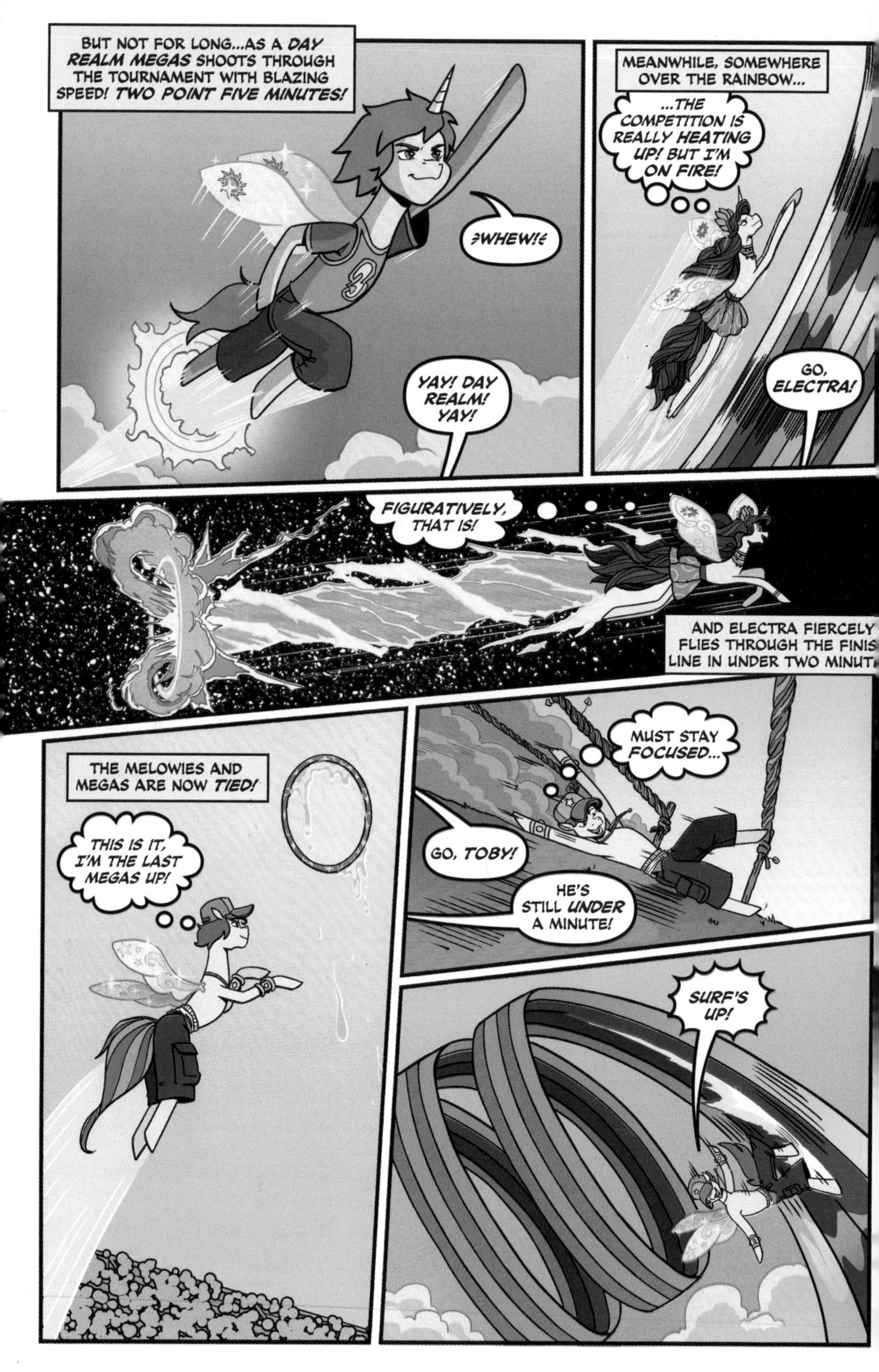
BUT NOT FOR LONG...AS A DAY REALM MEGAS SHOOTS THROUGH THE TOURNAMENT WITH BLAZING SPEED! TWO POINT FIVE MINUTES!
WHEW!
YAY! DAY REALM! YAY!
MEANWHILE, SOMEWHERE OVER THE RAINBOW...
...THE COMPETITION IS REALLY HEATING UP! BUT I'M ON FIRE!
GO, ELECTRA!
FIGURATIVELY, THAT IS!
AND ELECTRA FIERCELY FLIES THROUGH THE FINIS LINE IN UNDER TWO MINUT
THE MELOWIES AND MEGAS ARE NOW TIED!
THIS IS IT, I'M THE LAST MEGAS UP!
MUST STAY FOCUSED...
GO, TOBY!
HE'S STILL UNDER A MINUTE!
SURF'S UP!

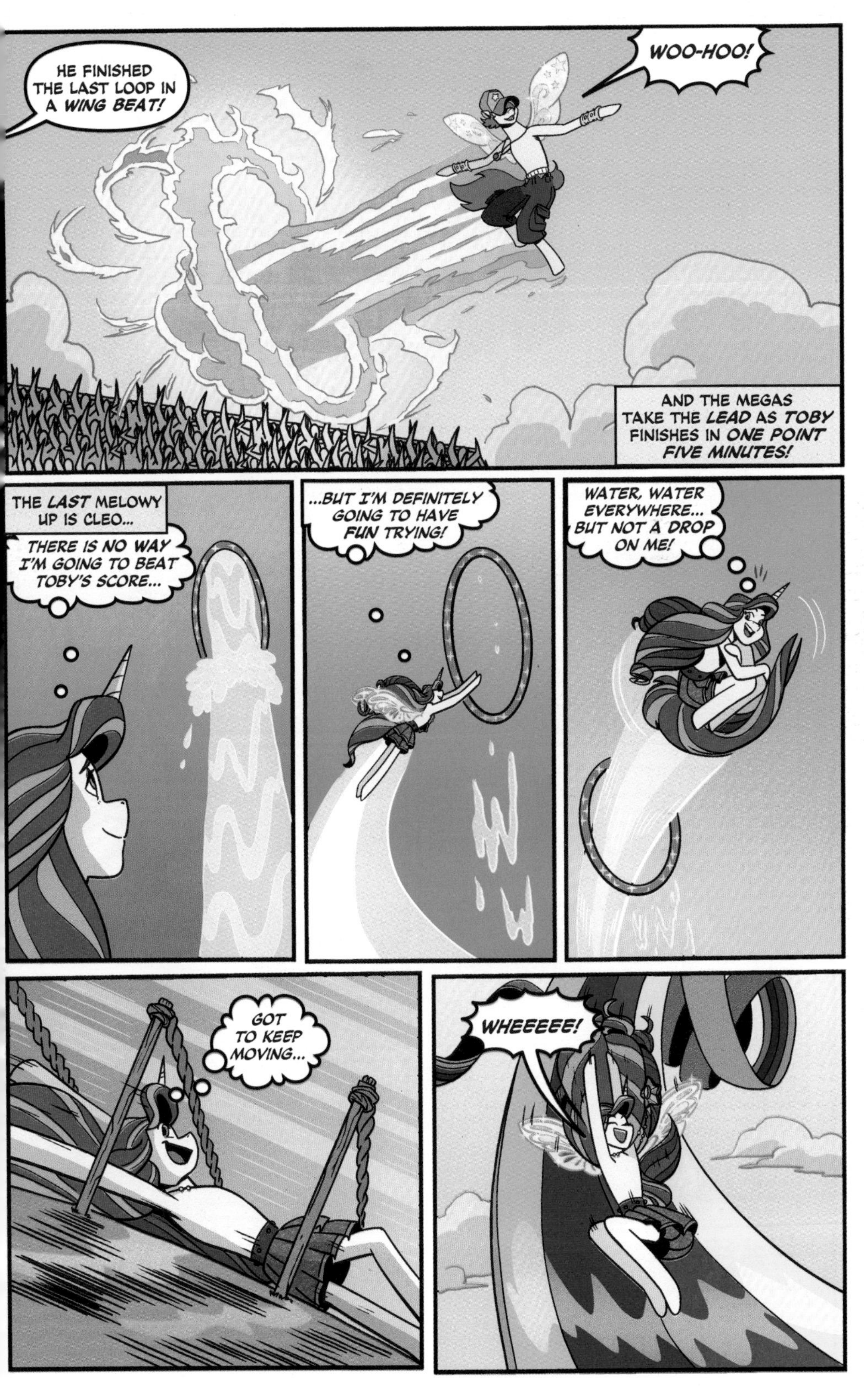
HE FINISHED THE LAST LOOP IN A WING BEAT!
WOO-HOO!
AND THE MEGAS TAKE THE LEAD AS TOBY FINISHES IN ONE POINT FIVE MINUTES!
THE LAST MELOWY UP IS CLEO...
THERE IS NO WAY I'M GOING TO BEAT TOBY'S SCORE...
...BUT I'M DEFINITELY GOING TO HAVE FUN TRYING!
WATER, WATER EVERYWHERE... BUT NOT A DROP ON ME!
GOT TO KEEP MOVING...
WHEEEEE!

WOOOOOOOOOO!
WOOOOOOOOOOO!
WHAT?
AND CLEO FINISHES IN UNDER ONE MINUTE!
OH, MY GOSH! I CAN'T BELIEVE IT!
WE CAN!
THE MELOWIES ARE THE WINNERS OF THE FIRST CHALLENGE, WITH CLEO SCORING THE BEST SPEED AND BEST PERFORMANCE!
YAAAAAAAY!
WOOOOOOOOOO!
CLAP
CLAP
CONGRATS, CLEO...THAT WAS IMPRESSIVE!
THANKS, TOBY, YOU WEREN'T SO BAD YOURSELF...
CIRCE IS RIGHT...
THERE IS NOTHING WRONG WITH AN INNOCENT SPELL TO MAKE MY TALENT SHINE...

...BY BORROWING SOME OF CLEO'S...
...ALL I HAVE TO DO IS PLACE CLEO'S STRAND OF HAIR INSIDE THIS MAGICAL PENDANT...
...AND HER TALENTS WILL TRANSFER OVER TO ME...
...AFTER ALL, IT'LL TEACH HER TO BE MORE HUMBLE, LIKE CIRCE SAID.
A BIT LATER, IN DESTINY'S GARDEN, TOBY IS TEACHING CLEO SOME TRICKS ON HIS LIGHT BOARD!
HOW? IT'S SO UNSTEADY!
FIRST OF ALL, LET GO OF YOUR FEAR AND RELAX!
DEEP BREATHS...FIND YOUR BALANCE, AND THINK OF THE LIGHT BOARD AS AN EXTENSION OF YOURSELF...
O--KAY...
HOW CAN A MELOWY LIKE YOU BE AFRAID OF A LIGHT BOARD?
WHAT DO YOU MEAN?

YOU'RE ONE OF THE *BRAVEST* MELOWIES I HAVE EVER KNOWN.
THANK YOU, BUT I DON'T FEEL VERY BRAVE MOST OF THE TIME...
...I GUESS I'M AFRAID THAT ONE DAY EVERYONE IS GOING TO FIND OUT...
...I'M NOT A *REAL* MELOWY...
ONE THING I CAN TELL YOU FOR SURE... YOU ARE A *REAL* CLEO, AND THAT I WOULDN'T CHANGE YOU FOR ALL OF AURA!
THANK YOU...
I-I SUDDENLY DON'T FEEL VERY WELL...
WHAT'S WRONG?
I HAVE TO GO!
I-I SUDDENLY FEEL SO...EMPTY...
I CAN FLY YOU BACK TO YOUR DORM, OR TO THE *NURSE*?
DON'T WORRY ABOUT IT! JUST LEAVE ME *ALONE!*
EVERY WORD HE SAYS, MAKES ME FEEL SO...EMPTY!

HE MAKES THE EMPTINESS GROW! I NEED TO GET AWAY!
DON'T YOU HAVE ANYTHING BETTER TO DO THAN FOLLOW ME?!
TOBY? IS EVERYTHING OKAY?
OH, HI, ERIS. I DON'T KNOW. CLEO JUST STARTED ACTING STRANGE.
SHE TENDS TO DO THAT SOMETIMES. I WOULDN'T WORRY.
REALLY? I'VE NEVER SEEN HER LIKE THAT BEFORE...
SINCE YOU'RE FREE NOW, MAYBE WE COULD GO FOR SOME SMOOTHIES AT SUGAR AND SPICE CAFE?
UM...WELL, IT DOESN'T SEEM LIKE CLEO WANTS HELP FROM ME RIGHT NOW, ANYWAY...SO... SURE, I'LL GO WITH YOU.
GREAT! I'M GOING TO CHANGE REAL QUICK!
OKAY! MEET ME IN THE SPORTS ARENA WHEN YOU'RE READY.

BACK IN HER DORM, AS THE DARK EMPTINESS SPREADS...AND THE FLASHES OF A BLACK DIAMOND CONTINUE...
...ALONG WITH FLASHES OF A DARK CAVE SOMEWHERE...
...AND A MYSTERIOUS FIGURE...
SHE DOESN'T LOOK SO GOOD...
DID TOBY SAY SOMETHING STUPID?
CLEO, ARE YOU OKAY?
I'M FINE! I HAVE TO GO!
UM...WHERE DO YOU HAVE TO GO?
BUT WE WERE JUST ABOUT TO PICK OUT DRESSES FOR THE DANCE!
AND MAYA AND I MADE BROWNIES!

I SAID--
I HAVE TO GO!
MEANWHILE...
THIS SPELL IS WORKING LIKE A CHARM!
OW! WATCH IT!
I HEARD YOU WEREN'T FEELING SO GOOD--
GET OUT OF MY WAY! I HAVE TO GO!
GO WHERE?
I MUST GO TO THE SUPREME RULER!

SUPREME RULER?
IF I FOLLOW HER, I CAN FORGET ABOUT MY DATE WITH TOBY!
BUT IF I DON'T, WHO KNOWS WHAT COULD HAPPEN?!
IF I GET HER TO TURN BACK SOON, MAYBE THERE WILL BE ENOUGH TIME LEFT TO GO OUT WITH TOBY.
CLEO! DON'T YOU WANT TO REST BEFORE THE BIG CHALLENGE TOMORROW?
UM...I DON'T THINK WE'VE EVER BEEN THIS FAR AWAY FROM THE DESTINY...

WHERE ARE WE?
THIS IS GETTING SCARY!
I DON'T THINK WE SHOULD GO IN THERE! LET'S GO BACK...NOW!
SUDDENLY, A HAUNTING VOICE ECHOS FROM WITHIN THE CAVE...
CLEO, COME TO ME... COME TO ME...
PLEASE... REVERSE THIS SPELL!

THIS BELONGS TO YOU! PLEASE TAKE IT!
E-ERIS, WHY DO YOU HAVE A STRAND OF MY HAIR...?
IT WORKED! THE SPELL IS BROKEN!
...AND WHERE IN ALL OF AURA, ARE WE?
I CAN EXPLAIN, BUT WE NEED TO LEAVE NOW!
A LITTLE LATER...
SO, YOU ARE TELLING ME THAT I HIT MY HEAD AND WANDERED OFF...
I DON'T THINK SO... WHY WOULD YOU HAVE A STRAND OF MY HAIR? THIS WAS PART OF A MAGIC SPELL!
FINE...I MAY HAVE PERFORMED AN INNOCENT SPELL...
ERIS!

I GOT JEALOUS OF TOBY LIKING YOU OVER ME...BUT I HAD NO IDEA THAT IT WAS GOING TO SEND YOU TO A STRANGE PLACE IN THE MIDDLE OF NOWHERE!
HOW COULD YOU DO SOMETHING SO TERRIBLE?
BUT I REVERSED IT!
JUST STAY AWAY FROM ME!
HEY, GUYS.
CLEO!
WE WERE SO WORRIED!
I'M SORRY IF I WAS ACTING STRANGE EARLIER...
...I HIT MY HEAD ON SOMETHING DURING THE TOURNAMENT AND IT MUST HAVE MESSED ME UP, BUT I FEEL MUCH BETTER NOW.
REALLY? I DIDN'T NOTICE THAT AT ALL!
BUT WE ARE SO RELIEVED TO SEE THAT YOU ARE BETTER NOW!

HONESTLY, I DON'T REALLY REMEMBER MUCH, WAS I TERRIBLE?
NAH!
ALL IS FORGOTTEN ANYWAY!
I KNOW THAT I'VE BEEN GROUCHY MORE THAN ONCE!
WHAT ARE FRIENDS FOR? FORGIVE AND FORGET!
I'M SO LUCKY TO HAVE THE MOST AMAZING FRIENDS!
...BY THE WAY, WHO'S WEARING THAT TO THE DANCE? IT'S BEAUTIFUL!
WE WERE HOPING YOU WOULD!
WE SAW THIS DRESS AT SATIN...
SO WE ALL PITCHED IN!
AND KNEW IT WAS MADE FOR YOU!
LATER IN THE NIGHT...LONG AFTER THE CASTLE'S LIGHTS GO OUT, AND DEEP IN THE DARKNESS... CIRCE IS PLANNING SOMETHING...
I SHOULDN'T HAVE TRUSTED A SMELLOWY TO DO MAGIC OF THE DARK.
"THIS WAS NO INNOCENT SPELL" SHE SAID...

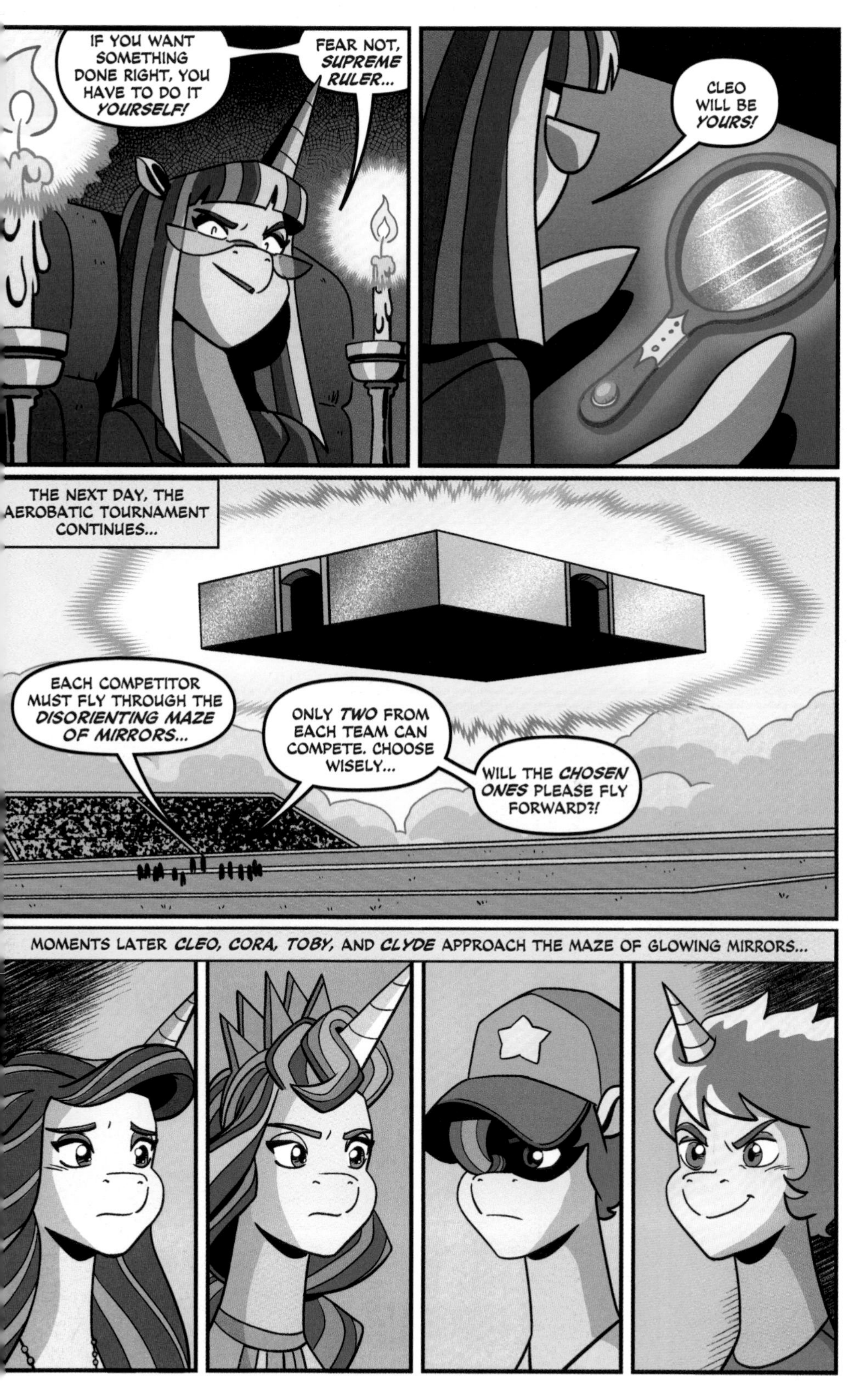
IF YOU WANT SOMETHING DONE RIGHT, YOU HAVE TO DO IT YOURSELF!
FEAR NOT, SUPREME RULER...
CLEO WILL BE YOURS!
THE NEXT DAY, THE AEROBATIC TOURNAMENT CONTINUES...
EACH COMPETITOR MUST FLY THROUGH THE DISORIENTING MAZE OF MIRRORS...
ONLY TWO FROM EACH TEAM CAN COMPETE. CHOOSE WISELY...
WILL THE CHOSEN ONES PLEASE FLY FORWARD?!
MOMENTS LATER CLEO, CORA, TOBY, AND CLYDE APPROACH THE MAZE OF GLOWING MIRRORS...

YOUR GOAL IS TO LOOK FOR THE MAGIC MIRROR AT THE END OF THE MAZE, AND FLY INTO IT...
EVERYTHING IS GOING ACCORDING TO PLAN...
THE MELOWY THAT FLIES THROUGH FIRST, IS THE WINNER!
TIME TO FLY, FILLIES!
CLEO WILL FLY THROUGH, AND DARKNESS WILL WIN!
WOW! THIS MAZE IS AMAZING!

MY REFLECTION SEEMS TO GO ON FOREVER! I WONDER HOW CORA IS DOING IN THE BLUE MAZE...?
WHICH WAY DO I GO NOW? EVERY PATH LOOKS THE SAME!
THIS IS PRETTY COOL!
CLEO?
CORA?
CLEO! STAY THERE! I'M COMING...
BUT I'M ON MY WAY TO YOU!

OW!
WHERE DID YOU GO?
BUMP
YOU'RE A TRICKER!
OW!
BUMP
SHE'S NOT THERE! IT'S JUST ANOTHER MIRROR!
GET IT TOGETHER, CORA!
THAT WASN'T EXACTLY MINDFUL!
AND NOW I'M TALKING TO MY SELVES!
I KNOW THINGS ARE NOT GREAT BETWEEN US RIGHT NOW, CLEO...AND THAT YOU CAN'T HEAR ME RIGHT NOW...
...BUT I WOULD LOVE IT... IF YOU WOULD GO TO THE DANCE WITH ME...
IT LOOKS LIKE WE ARE ALL GOING IN THE SAME DIRECTION...

THERE'S THE MAGIC MIRROR!
YAY!
WHAT THE--?! WHERE DID THAT WATERFALL COME FROM?
THERE'S NO WAY I CAN GET THROUGH THAT WITHOUT GETTING WET!
IS THIS SUPPOSED TO HAPPEN?
LOOKS LIKE I'M NOT THE ONLY ONE THAT'S CONFUSED!
WAIT! CLEO'S NOT HERE! DID SHE GET THROUGH THE WATERFALL?

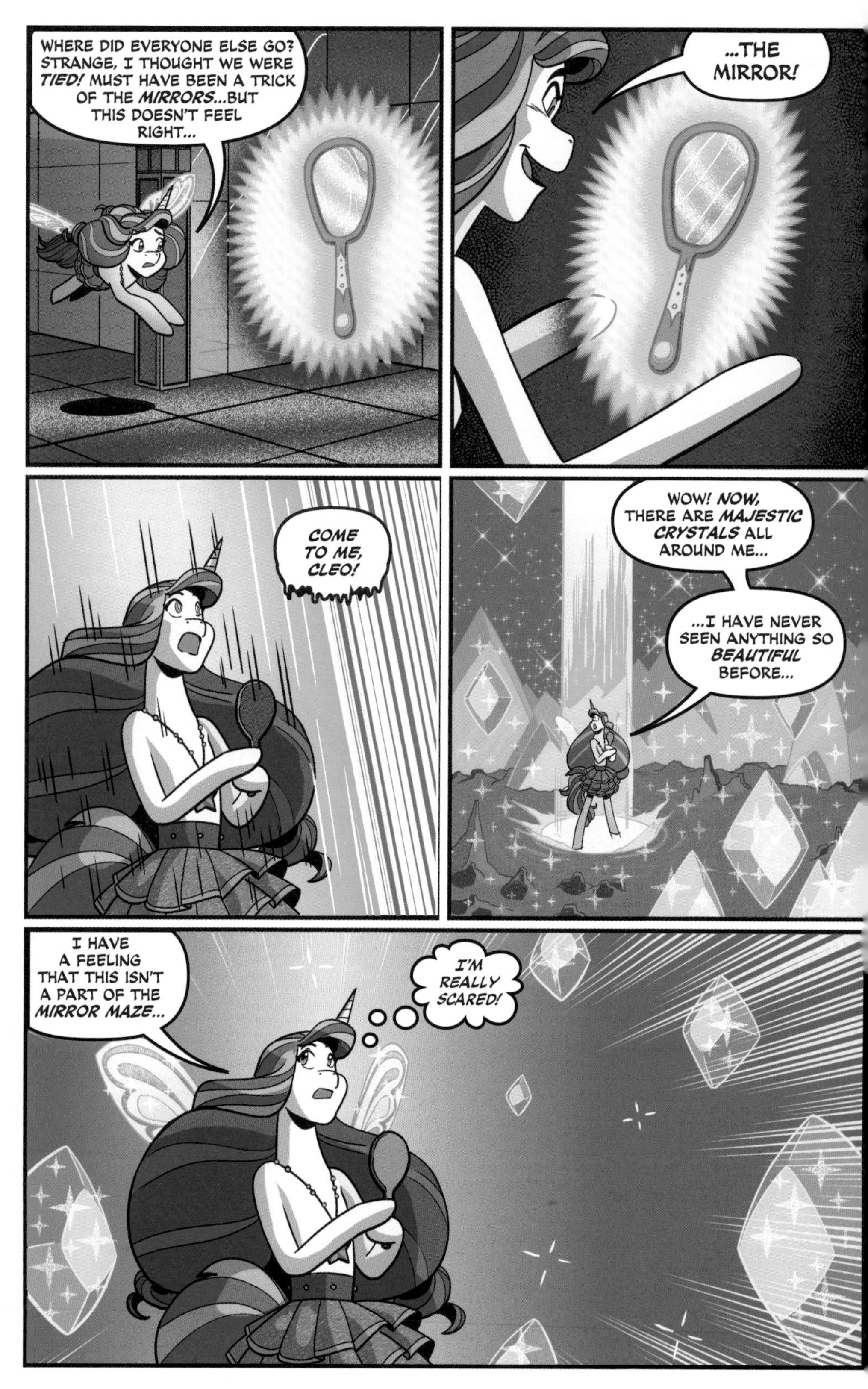
WHERE DID EVERYONE ELSE GO? STRANGE, I THOUGHT WE WERE TIED! MUST HAVE BEEN A TRICK OF THE MIRRORS...BUT THIS DOESN'T FEEL RIGHT...
...THE MIRROR!
COME TO ME, CLEO!
WOW! NOW, THERE ARE MAJESTIC CRYSTALS ALL AROUND ME...
...I HAVE NEVER SEEN ANYTHING SO BEAUTIFUL BEFORE...
I HAVE A FEELING THAT THIS ISN'T A PART OF THE MIRROR MAZE...
I'M REALLY SCARED!

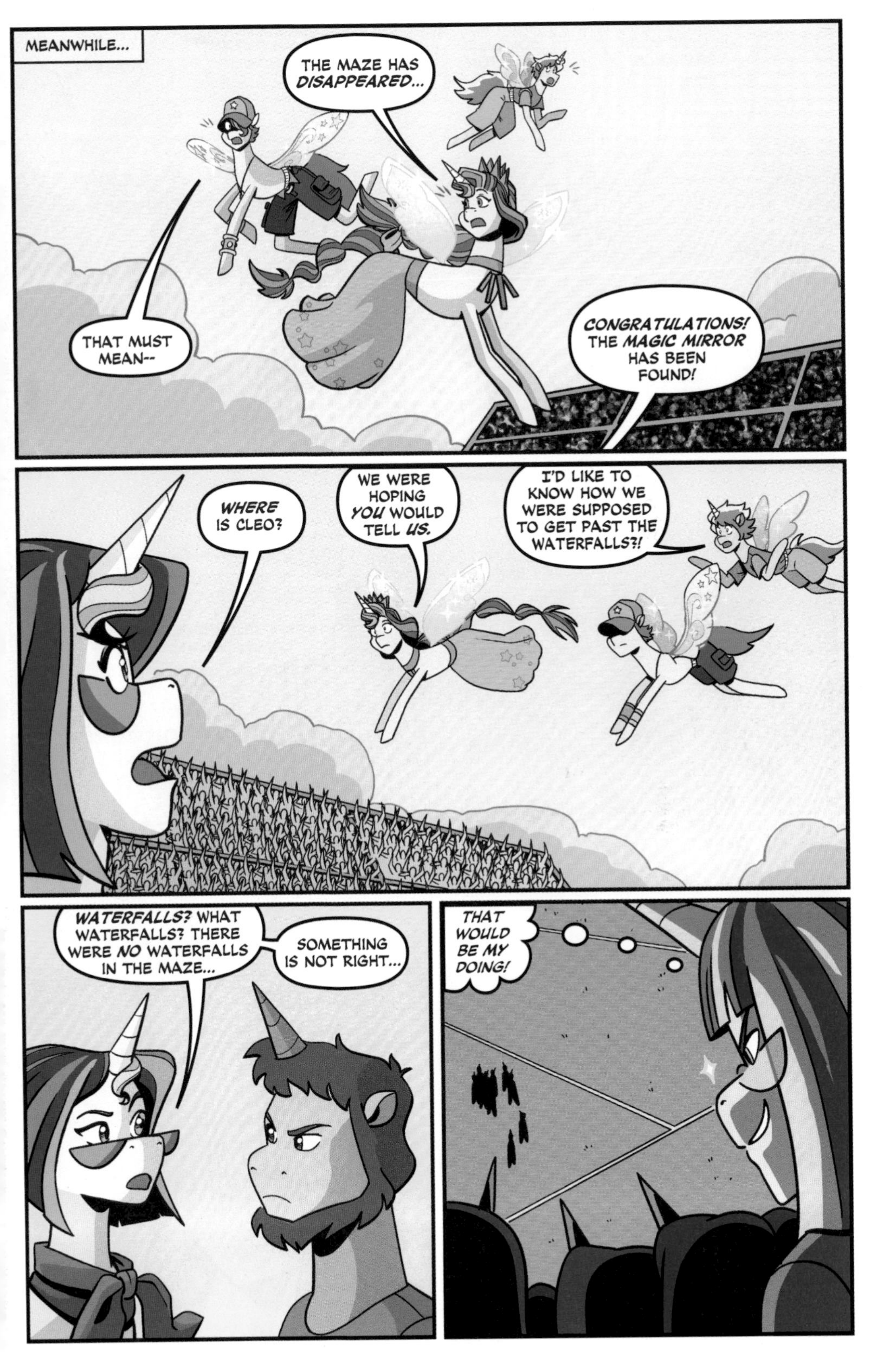
MEANWHILE...
THE MAZE HAS DISAPPEARED...
THAT MUST MEAN--
CONGRATULATIONS! THE MAGIC MIRROR HAS BEEN FOUND!
WHERE IS CLEO?
WE WERE HOPING YOU WOULD TELL US.
I'D LIKE TO KNOW HOW WE WERE SUPPOSED TO GET PAST THE WATERFALLS?!
WATERFALLS? WHAT WATERFALLS? THERE WERE NO WATERFALLS IN THE MAZE...
SOMETHING IS NOT RIGHT...
THAT WOULD BE MY DOING!

PRINCIPAL GIA, WE NEED YOUR ASSISTANCE!
I'M SO CONFUSED. WE WON, RIGHT?
I DON'T THINK THAT IS IMPORTANT RIGHT NOW...
?!
ATTENTION STUDENTS, UNTIL WE FIND THE WHEREABOUTS OF CLEO, THE TOURNAMENT HAS BEEN SUSPENDED...
IF ANY TEACHER OR STUDENT HAS AN INKLING OF WHERE CLEO COULD BE, PLEASE COME FORWARD!
WHAT IS GOING ON, SELENA? WHERE COULD CLEO HAVE GONE?
I DON'T KNOW, MAYA...
I MIGHT KNOW...
ERIS...?

CLEO, I'VE BEEN WAITING A LONG TIME FOR SOMEONE LIKE YOU.
WH-WHO IS *THAT?*
DO NOT *FEAR*... I'M NOT GOING TO HARM YOU.
I WANT TO HELP YOU...
UM... HELP ME?
WHERE IS YOUR *SYMBOL?*
WHICH *REALM* DO YOU COME FROM?
UM... I DON'T KNOW...

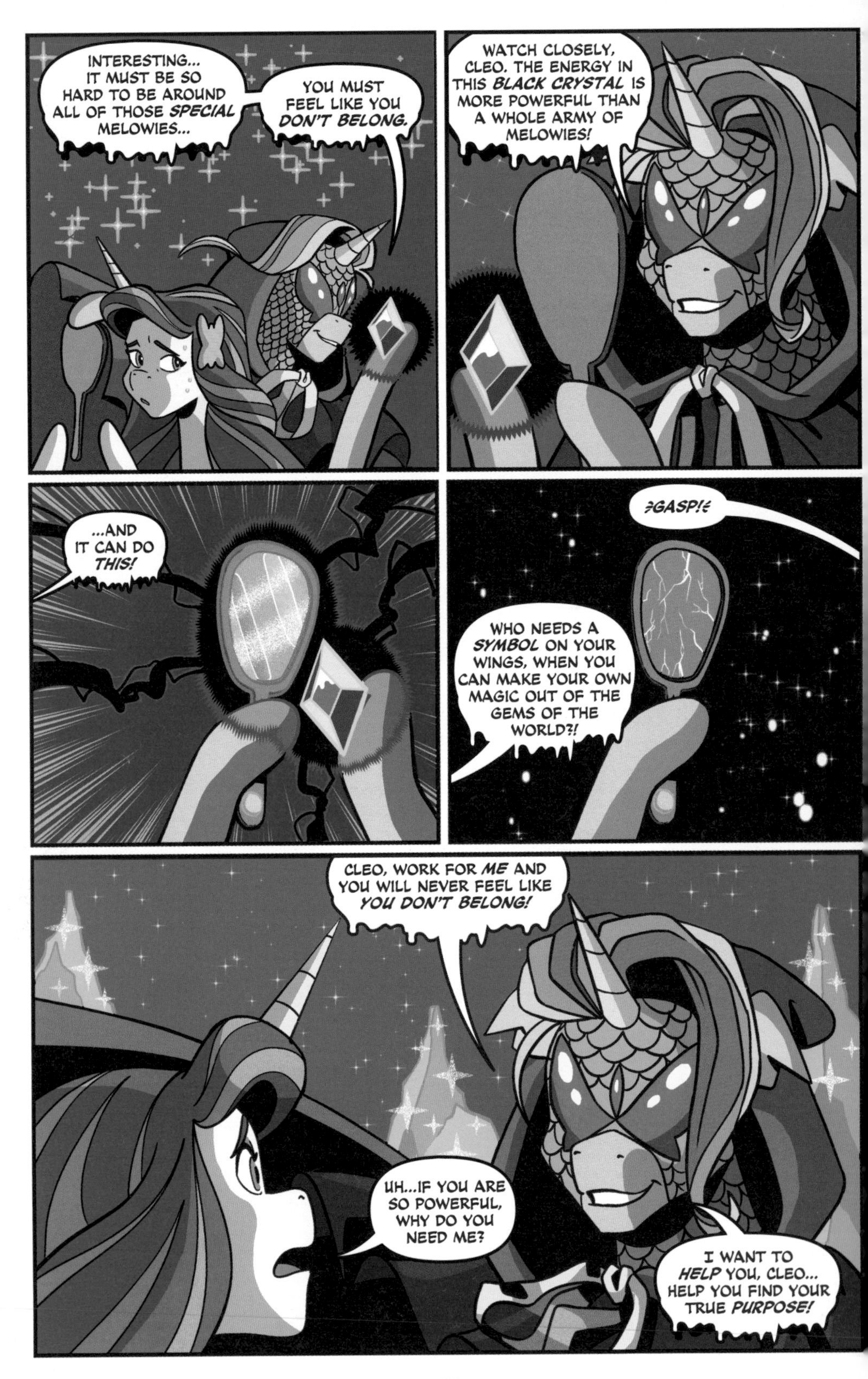
INTERESTING... IT MUST BE SO HARD TO BE AROUND ALL OF THOSE *SPECIAL* MELOWIES...
YOU MUST FEEL LIKE YOU *DON'T BELONG.*
WATCH CLOSELY, CLEO. THE ENERGY IN THIS *BLACK CRYSTAL* IS MORE POWERFUL THAN A WHOLE ARMY OF MELOWIES!
...AND IT CAN DO *THIS!*
GASP!
WHO NEEDS A *SYMBOL* ON YOUR WINGS, WHEN YOU CAN MAKE YOUR OWN MAGIC OUT OF THE GEMS OF THE WORLD?!
CLEO, WORK FOR *ME* AND YOU WILL NEVER FEEL LIKE *YOU DON'T BELONG!*
UH...IF YOU ARE SO POWERFUL, WHY DO YOU NEED ME?
I WANT TO *HELP* YOU, CLEO... HELP YOU FIND YOUR TRUE *PURPOSE!*

WE BELONG TOGETHER! AND TOGETHER WE CAN MAKE A WORLD FOR OUR KIND!
...A WORLD WITHOUT MELOWIES!
THAT DOESN'T SOUND LIKE A NICE WORLD TO ME!
YOU HAVE SO MUCH POTENTIAL, CLEO, AND I CAN MAKE YOUR MAGIC SHINE!
MIGHT AS WELL TURN ME INTO A CRYSTAL, I WILL NEVER BETRAY MY FRIENDS!
VERY WELL, I'LL HOLD ONTO THIS IN YOUR MEMORY... HAHAHAHA!
THE POWER IS MINE...
MY STAR NECKLACE!
DON'T WORRY, YOUR FRIENDS WILL JOIN YOU SOON IN THE REALM OF ETERNAL DARKNESS...
SAY GOODBYE TO MAGIC FOREVER!
GASP! WHAT?! NO!

SUDDENLY, OTHERS ARRIVE IN THE CRYSTAL CAVE...
YOU WERE *RIGHT*, ERIS! THERE SHE IS! WE'VE FOUND CLEO!
MY MINIONS! COME OUT OF THE SHADOWS AND *DESTROY THEM!*
WE MAY *OUTNUMBER* THE *DARK FORCES*, BUT THEIR WANDS ARE *POWERFUL!*

MEANWHILE, PRINCIPAL GIA IS READY TO FIGHT THE RULER OF DARKNESS...
STILL THINK YOU DISARMED ME, GIA?! I HAVE THE STAR!
CLEO! I'M SO GLAD YOU'RE OKAY!
THIS PLACE IS NOT SAFE! WE ALL NEED TO LEAVE BEFORE THE CAVE COLLAPSES!
NOT YET...THAT EVIL PEGASUS, HAS MY STAR NECKLACE!
THERE IS ONE DETAIL YOU ARE MISSING...
NO! STOP! STOP!
THE STAR SERVES ONE PURPOSE...
NO! IT'S MINE! COME BACK!

"...TO PROTECT THE KEEPER."
...ME?
I LOVE WHEN THIS HAPPENS!
CLEO'S MAGIC SHINES THROUGH ME... AND HER FRIENDS...
...AND WILL DEFEAT THESE EVIL MINIONS!
THE SUPREME RULER HAS VANISHED!
KRESH
KRESH
RUMMBLE
KRAK
WHERE DID THE MINIONS GO?!
IT'S TIME TO FLY OUT, THE CAVE IS COLLAPSING!
RUMBLE

DID EVERYONE MAKE IT OUT?! LEAVE NO MELOWIES BEHIND!
KRESHH
JUST SO YOU KNOW, I TOLD PRINCIPAL GIA EVERYTHING! I KNOW YOU DON'T BELIEVE ME, BUT I DO REGRET CASTING *THAT SPELL!*
ERIS, YOU SAVED *MY LIFE!*
EVERYTHING ELSE IS *FORGIVEN* AND *FORGOTTEN!*
I DID? I HAD NO CHOICE, BUT TO TELL THEM ABOUT THE CAVE!
YOU ALWAYS HAVE A *CHOICE!* YOU'RE A *TRUE FRIEND,* AND A *TRUE MELOWY!*
WHO WERE THOSE *TERRIBLE PEGASUS?*
...AND WHAT DID THEY WANT WITH CLEO?!
HONESTLY, I DON'T EXACTLY KNOW...BUT I *DO* KNOW WHAT THEY WANT...

THEY WANT TO TURN AURA INTO ONE REALM...
...A REALM OF DARKNESS!
BUT DO NOT WORRY... AS LONG AS THERE ARE MELOWIES LIKE US...
...LIGHT WILL ALWAYS WIN!
LATER, BACK AT THE DESTINY SPORTS ARENA...
THIS HAS BEEN A TRYING TIME FOR US ALL, BUT DO NOT FEAR...
YOU ARE ALL PROTECTED!
THE BEST THING YOU CAN DO NOW, IS KEEP GROWING AS MELOWIES AND MEGAS... THAT SAID, OUR LAST CHALLENGE SHALL BEGIN!
THE FINAL CHALLENGE, IS A SOLO PERFORMANCE...AND CLEO IS CHOSEN BY HER TEAM TO REPRESENT THEM...
I CALL THIS DARK AND LIGHT.
CLEO DOES AN INTERPRETIVE FLYING PERFORMANCE...

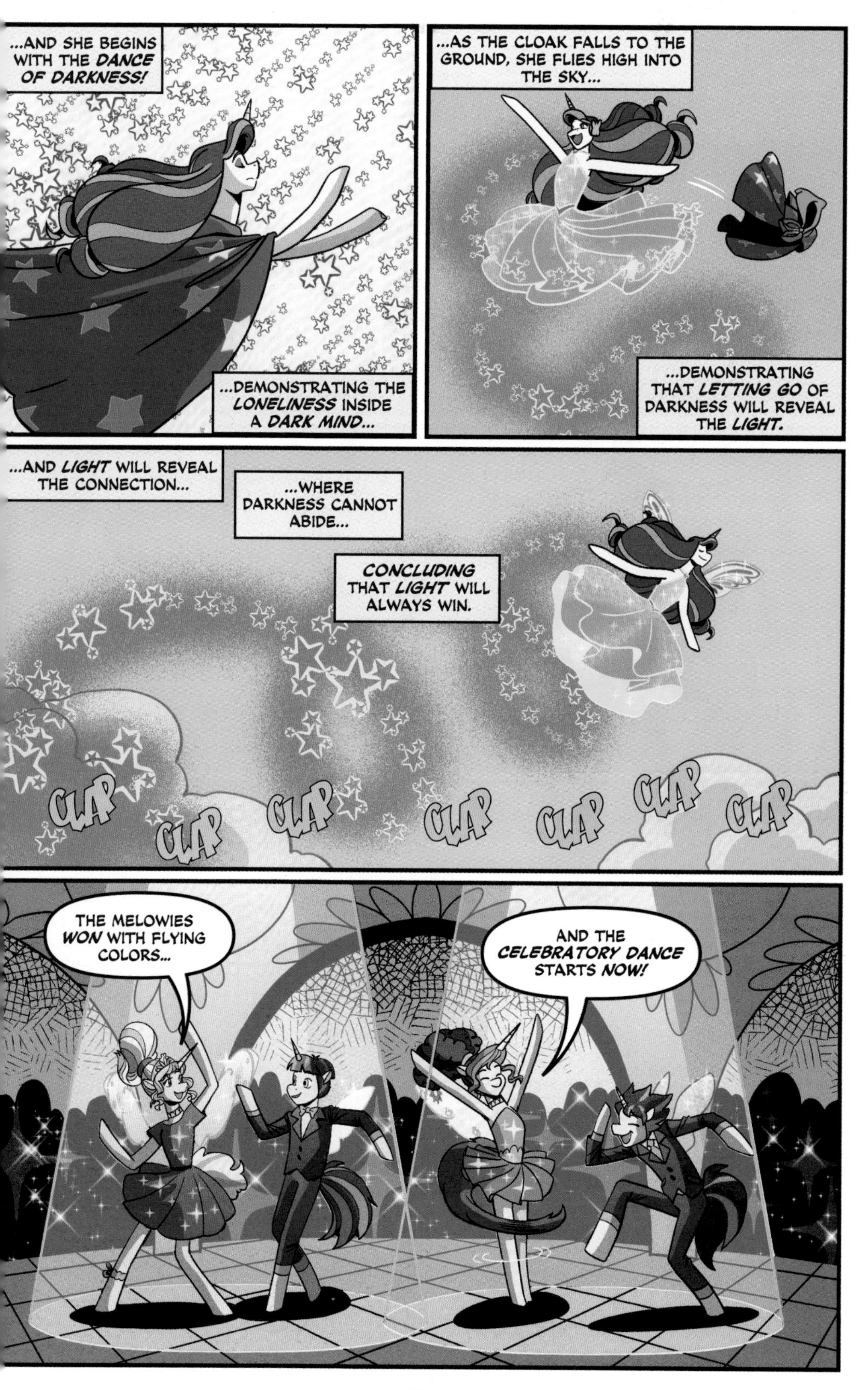
...AND SHE BEGINS WITH THE DANCE OF DARKNESS!
...DEMONSTRATING THE LONELINESS INSIDE A DARK MIND...
...AS THE CLOAK FALLS TO THE GROUND, SHE FLIES HIGH INTO THE SKY...
...DEMONSTRATING THAT LETTING GO OF DARKNESS WILL REVEAL THE LIGHT.
...AND LIGHT WILL REVEAL THE CONNECTION...
...WHERE DARKNESS CANNOT ABIDE...
CONCLUDING THAT LIGHT WILL ALWAYS WIN.
CLAP
CLAP
CLAP
CLAP
CLAP
CLAP
CLAP
THE MELOWIES WON WITH FLYING COLORS...
AND THE CELEBRATORY DANCE STARTS NOW!

NICE DANCING, AERIES!
YOU MELOWIES MIGHT HAVE WON THE FLYING CHALLENGE, BUT I GOT THE DANCING MOVES!
HEY, DANCE WITH ME!
UM...SURE.
HAS ANYONE SEEN CLEO?!
DON'T WORRY, I HAVEN'T SEEN TOBY EITHER!
HAHAHA!
I DON'T KNOW WHAT I WAS SO AFRAID OF BEFORE! WOOOOO!
AFRAID OF HAVING THE TIME OF YOUR LIFE... WOO-HOO!
END

WATCH OUT FOR PAPERCUTZ

elcome to the timely, talent-testing, third MELOWY graphic novel · "Coach" Cortney Powell and Ryan "Judge" Jampole based on e competitive characters created by "Drill Instructor" Danielle ll) Star, gamely brought to you by Papercutz, those winning folks dicated to publishing great graphic novels for all ages. I'm Jim licrup, the Editor-in-Chief and the Destiny Aerobatic Team mascot, re to talk about all things MELOWY and Papercutz…

eing the Aerobatic Tournament featured in this MELOWY graphic vel reminded us of the Olympics, which reminds us of another onderful Papercutz graphic novel,GERONIMO STILTON #10 eronimo Stilton Saves the Olympics." As you know, Geronimo the editor-in-chief of Mouse Island's *Rodent's Gazette*, and quite ten finds himself travelling back in time to save the future, by otecting the past – usually from those pesky Pirate Cats. Believe or not, the Pirate Cats thought they could change history by nning the first Olympics back in 1894, but Geronimo was not out to let that happen. He went so far as to actually compete in at premiere Olympics himself!

d how could I forget about another Papercutz graphic novel, THE MURFS #11 "The Smurf Olympics," where we got to see our little ue buddies compete in lots of Olympic events? Turns out those ys are incredibly competitive. In SMURFS THE VILLAGE BEHIND E WALL #2 "The Betrayal of Smurfblossom," we see the female murfs (introduced in the movie *Smurfs: The Lost Village*) compete the Great Smurf Tree Games. Things get really interesting hen the Smurfy Grove champion is challenged by Handy Smurf. rhaps the most unexpected competition of all takes place in THE MURFS #25 "The Gambling Smurfs," when the Smurfs Village is reatened to be destroyed to make room for a casino, and Papa murf enlists Gargamel to represent the Smurfs in a tournament ainst these scoundrels. The results are surprising and hilarious.

en if you're not a Melowy, a Smurf, or even a mouse, it's easy to t caught up with the competitive side of life. Whether it's being volved in sports, pageants, playing video games, getting good ades, or whatever challenges you may face, the thing to always member is to simply try to be the best you that you can be. llow your own interests. Just like the Melowies, you can attend hool and discover what your true power is. One of the little things enjoyed about "Time to Fly" was how supportive Cleo's friends ere of her, well, all of them except Eris. Instead of being jealous of r success, they were happy for her. Competition can be healthy, d bring the best out of us, or in some cases it could bring out the orst (Looking at you, Eris!).

peaking of competition, do you realize how many people and mpanies are competing just for your attention? Bet you didn't alize how important you are! Every day you're bombarded with commercials trying to get you to see certain TV shows or movies, eat breakfast cereals or Happy Meals, play with specific dolls or video games. Even when you go to a bookstore or library, hundreds of books are trying to get your attention so that you'll read them. At Papercutz we're also competing to get your attention – we do it by publishing the best graphic novels we possibly can. Here's an example of how competition focuses us on making sure we do our very best, to be worthy of your attention. We also do things such as attend Book Shows to get the word out about Papercutz graphic novels. Cortney Powell and Ryan Jampole were at a recent Brooklyn Book Festival in New York City, and loved meeting all the MELOWY fans who came by the Papercutz booth. And we want you to know we're very thankful that you're spending some of your valuable time with us.

Cortney "Coach" Powell   Ryan "Judge" Jampole

And what better way to conclude this mini-essay on competition, than by previewing THE SMURFS #25 "The Gambling Smurfs" and GERONIMO STILTON REPORTER #2 "It's My Scoop!," about the competition between Geronimo's newspaper and its rival, *The Daily Rat*. Seems like someone's been stealing Geronimo's scoops! See what we're talking about on the following pages.

Oh, we know we promised to include bios of MELOWY colorist Laurie E. Smith and letterer Wilson Ramos Jr. in this Watch Out for Papercutz column, but we had to reschedule it for MELOWY #4 "Frozen in Time," which is coming to your favorite bookseller or library soon. And there's even more we'd like to tell you about, but we're afraid it's time to fly!

Thanks, Jim

STAY IN TOUCH!

EMAIL:	salicrup@papercutz.com
WEB:	papercutz.com
TWITTER:	@papercutzgn
INSTAGRAM:	@papercutzgn
FACEBOOK:	PAPERCUTZGRAPHICNOVELS
FANMAIL:	Papercutz, 160 Broadway, Suite 700, East Wing, New York, NY 10038

Here's a special preview of GERONIMO STILTON REPORTER #2 "It's My Scoop!"

LATER, BACK AT THE RODENT'S GAZETTE...
I CAN'T BELIEVE IT!
I WAS SCOOPED BY SIMON SQUEALER POSING AS ME!
HOW'D HE KNOW THAT THE NEW MAYOR WAS GIVING YOU THE EXCLUSIVE?
I DON'T KNOW, BUT THIS IS EXACTLY THE KIND OF UNDERHANDED TACTIC I'D EXPECT FROM SIMON'S BOSS, SALLY RATMOUSEN!
BIP
BIP
BIP
HEADS UP! NEWSFLASH ON MY BEN PAD!
BIP

NOW MY BIG STORY ON THE CITY'S CENTENNIAL CELEBRATION IS NOTHING MORE THAN TABLOID TRASH!
SALLY RATMOUSEN HERE WITH THE NEWS SO HOT IT'LL SINGE YOUR FUR!
ONLY THE DAILY RAT HAS THE SCOOP FROM THE NEW MAYOR HIMSELF ON THE NEW MOUSE CITY'S ONE-HUNDRED-YEAR ANNIVERSARY CELEBRATION!
OH! THE CELEBRATION IS GOING TO BE SUPER BIG! BIGGER THAN SUPER BIG!
AND WE'VE GOT A **SUPER-SECRET CELEBRITY** TO HOST!
OF COURSE, I CAN'T TELL YOU WHO IT'S GOING TO BE, BUT IT'LL BE SUPER, AND BIG! **HA HA HA HA!**

Here's a special bonus preview of THE SMURFS #25 "The Gambling Smurfs"...

Good try! Last one there's a smurf!
Ha! Ha! Ha! I'm always first when Hefty Smurf's not around!
CHOKE! KOF! KOF! KOF!
?
Oooo... I'm sure Chef Smurf won't want to smurf me an extra dessert now!
ATCHOO!
Can you smurf me a little from your sack?
No way! Otherwise I'm the one risking not smurfing a dessert!
KOF KOF
AHA! KNAVE! YOUR FINAL HOUR HAS COME!
?
!?
?
You have no chance!
CLANG
!
© Peyo

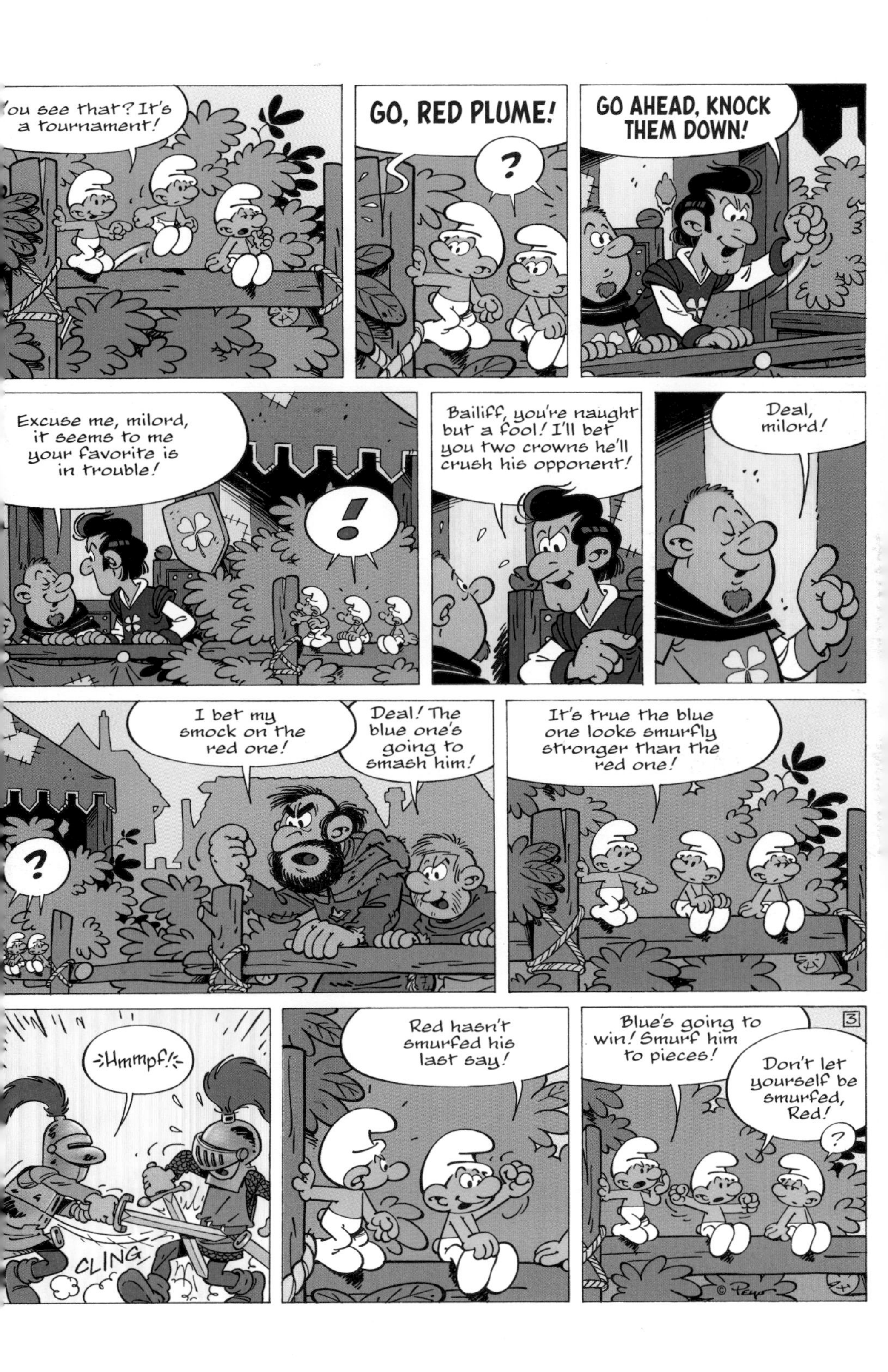
ou see that? It's a tournament!
GO, RED PLUME!
?
GO AHEAD, KNOCK THEM DOWN!
Excuse me, milord, it seems to me your favorite is in trouble!
!
Bailiff, you're naught but a fool! I'll bet you two crowns he'll crush his opponent!
Deal, milord!
I bet my smock on the red one!
Deal! The blue one's going to smash him!
?
It's true the blue one looks smurfly stronger than the red one!
Hmmpf!
CLING
Red hasn't smurfed his last say!
3
Blue's going to win! Smurf him to pieces!
Don't let yourself be smurfed, Red!
?
© Peyo

Don't miss THE SMURFS #25 "The Gambling Smurfs," available at booksellers and libraries now.

Map of Aura

The Spring Realm

The Winter Realm